# THE
# SMALL POTATOES
# AND
# THE MAGIC SHOW

## Harriet Ziefert and Jon Ziefert
### Illustrated by Richard Brown

**A Yearling Book**

Published by
Dell Publishing Co., Inc.
1 Dag Hammarskjold Plaza
New York, New York 10017

Yearling ® TM 913705, Dell Publishing Co., Inc.

ISBN: 0-440-48114-7

Printed in the United States of America
**Second Dell printing—August 1984**
CW

**Book Club Edition**

*For Beverly,*

*a charter member*

# CHAPTER ONE

# THE PICNIC

Hi. We're a group.

We have a club and a clubhouse.

We've named ourselves the SMALL
POTATOES.

Right now, we're off to a picnic!

You can come with us.

There's plenty of room.

Being a club member is great.

You can be a member too.

Come on, meet the gang.

I'll introduce you.

There's Roger, Sam, Chris,

Molly, Sue, Scott, and Spot.

Roger wears glasses. Sam has freckles.

Chris is tall and Molly is not.

Sue has braids and Scott does not.

And Spot is Spot. (He's also Molly's dog.)

We have boxes and bats, balls and bats—
and a blanket too!
We're looking for a good spot for our stuff.
Sam shouted, "I think I found a great place.
The ground is flat. We can spread the
blanket and take off our socks and shoes."
Everyone agreed Sam had found a good place.
Chris and Molly spread the blanket.
Spot sat in the middle while Sam put heavy
rocks on the corners.

"Let's eat our sandwiches now," said Chris.

"But we just got here," said Roger.

"If you're not hungry, you can wait," answered
    Chris. "But I'm eating right now!"

"Me too!" said Sam.

"Me too!" said Sue.

"Me too!" said Molly.

*"Arf! Arf!"* said Spot.

 Everybody started to eat.

"Oops! I dropped my jelly sandwich!" cried
    Molly.

"Call Spot," someone said. "He's good at
    cleaning up messes."

SPOT! SPOT! CAN YOU CLEAN THIS
    SPOT?

"Look," said Sue, "an inchworm is walking up
my arm."

"And a mosquito is drinking from my foot!"
cried Scott. "OUCH!"

"I think we'd better clean up before the ants
arrive!" said Roger.

The kids mumbled "okay" and crumpled up
their papers.

Molly and Scott found a basket for garbage.

"What should we do now?" asked Chris.

"I have an idea," said Roger. "Let's
　　play a game of hide-and-seek."

"I'll be 'IT,'" said Molly. "Hurry up and
　　let's get started."

Molly headed toward a big tree.

Everybody else began thinking of a direction
to run in after Molly had begun to count.

When Molly got to the tree, she hid her eyes.

"NO PEEKING!" shouted Sam.

"NO CHEATING!" yelled Sue.

"COUNT TO FIFTY," said Roger.

"AND COUNT SLOWLY!" said Sam.

"I'm ready!" shouted Molly.

She began to count:

"1, 2, 3, 4, 5, 6, 7, 8, 9 . . ."

By now almost everyone was out of sight.

Molly kept on counting:

"10, 11, 12, 13, 14, 15 . . ."

There were a few bushes moving, but that
was all.

Molly was almost done:

". . . 35, 36, 37, 38, 39, 40, 41,
42, 43, 44, 45, 46, 47, 48, 49 . . .
50! ANYONE AROUND MY BASE
IS IT!"

When Molly opened her eyes, it seemed as if she were all alone in the park.

# CHAPTER TWO

## SMART DOG

Molly ran in the direction of the duck pond.

But she didn't spot anybody—except Spot.

And he was chasing a cat.

When the cat ran up a tree, Spot ran
after Molly.

Molly really didn't mind Spot tagging
along. I won't be so lonely, she
thought.

Molly looked and looked, but she couldn't
find anybody.

She was getting upset.

Suddenly she bent down and whispered
something to Spot.

Spot was off!

He ran to some bushes.

He sniffed.

He found Roger and Sam.

Then Spot ran to a park bench.

He sniffed some more.

He found Sue.

When he stood in front of a statue and barked, out came the rest of the gang.

"You cheated," everyone shouted at Molly.

"This game was no fair!" Chris yelled.

Molly answered, "Spot's my dog and I played fair!"

"You can't play fair with a dog around," said Sue, "so let's play something else."

"Okay," said Chris, "does everyone remember how to play Spud?"

"Sure we do," said Roger, "we're not dumb!"

"So let's get started," said Chris.

"I'll give each of you a number. And keep your number a secret!"

Then Sue got the ball.

She threw it in the air and shouted:

"FIVE!"

Everyone ran—except Roger.
Roger's number was five and he had
to catch the ball.
When he caught it, he yelled "SPUD!"

Everyone stopped when they heard "SPUD!"
Roger took three steps and tried to
hit Sam with the ball.
Roger threw and missed!
So Roger had "S."

Now Roger threw the ball in the air
and shouted: "THREE!"
That was Scott's number.
Scott ran for the ball.
But so did Spot.
Who got the ball?
Of course—it was Spot!
Spot would not give the ball to Scott.
Scott said, "Molly, would you please come
here and talk to this dog!"

Molly bent over and whispered into
Spot's ear.
Spot listened, then he smiled and ran away.
Spot always seemed to understand just
what Molly was saying.

# CHAPTER THREE

# THE PASSWORD

"I'm tired!" said Roger.

"Me too!" said Sue.

"What a day!" said Sam. "Let's head
    back to the clubhouse."

Roger, Sam, Chris,

Molly, Sue, Scott—

they all walked together.

Chris, who always seemed to be thinking

about food, shouted:

"Look, there's the ice cream man!

Let's go get some before the truck

drives away."

We all ran in the direction of the parked

truck.

"What'll you have, kids?" asked the ice cream
man.

"I want a double chocolate fudge pop," said
Molly.

"So do I," said Roger.

"I want a Creamsicle," said Scott, licking his
lips.

"We want vanilla cones," said Sue and Sam.

"And I'll have an ice cream sandwich," said
Chris.

Everyone in our club just loves ice cream.
What's your favorite kind?

We finished our ice cream quickly.

Then we walked slowly toward our clubhouse.

When we got there, Chris shouted:

"SPOT BEAT US HOME!"

"Spot did exactly what I told him to do,"
said Molly. "I sent him to the clubhouse
so he wouldn't bother us anymore."

"Can we have a meeting?" asked Sue.

"If it's short!" grumbled Roger.

The meeting came to order.

Sam stood up and said:

"I've been thinking. This club is missing something. We're missing something very important."

Everyone wondered what was missing.

The club had members.

The club had membership cards.

The club had a clubhouse.

What else did it need?

"We need a password," said Sam.

"Who has an idea?"

Everyone was quiet.

"Whoever has an idea, speak up!" said Sue.

But no one said anything.

Finally Chris stood up.

He said, "I think I know a good word."

Chris did not want to say the word out loud,

so he walked around and whispered it

into each person's ear.

Roger, Sam, Molly,
Sue, Scott, and Spot—
they liked the word a lot.
They promised to keep it a secret.
(Since you can keep a secret too,
Spot will tell you the password
for the SMALL POTATOES CLUB).

# CHAPTER FOUR

## A MONEY-MAKING IDEA

"This club needs to earn money," said Sue.

"So how can we raise some?" asked Sam.

No one answered too quickly.

"We can sell lemonade," said Roger.

"Too boring!" answered Molly.

"We can have a car wash," said Sue.

"Too wet!" said Scott.

"Doesn't anybody have a really good idea?"
    complained Roger.

"I do!" said Chris. "I have the best idea."

"Well, what's your great idea?" Roger asked.

Chris answered, "My idea is a magic show.
We can build a stage right in front of
our clubhouse."

"Wish you lots of luck," mumbled Roger.

"Do you really think we could do it?" asked
Scott.

"Sure we can," said Chris.

"How much can we charge?" someone asked.

"Fifty cents!" said Molly. "We need the money!"

"Well, for fifty cents," said Sam, "each one of us had better learn a really good trick!"

"*Arf! Arf!*" said Spot, agreeing with Sam.

Chris said, "I think we should vote about the magic show. Yesses stand up and nos stay down."

Everyone stood up except Roger.

There were five yesses, one no, plus one bow-wow.

So Chris said, "Okay, we'll have the show!"

"The meeting is over now," said Molly. "It's almost dinnertime and Spot wants to go home."

Sue said, "Let's meet tomorrow right after breakfast. Tonight think about magic tricks!"

# CHAPTER FIVE

# GETTING READY

We started early the next day.

We needed a stage, a table, old sheets,

wooden boards, and all kinds of props.

Luckily someone had a magic wand.

We had lots to do and we worked hard.

"I learned two card tricks," said Roger.

"I couldn't learn any!" complained Chris.
"Will you teach me one?"

"Sure," said Roger.

Roger got a regular deck of cards.

Then he looked at Chris and said,
"Pick a card."

Chris picked a card.

Roger told him to put the card in the middle
of the deck.

Then Roger said, "I'm going to tell you the
secret of this trick. I peeked at the
bottom card in the deck before I started."

"Does every trick have a secret?" asked Chris.

"Sure," said Molly, "even the mind-reading
trick that I learned has one!"

"Then, to be a great magician, I just have
to learn a secret!" exclaimed Chris.

"We're going to perform the most spectacular
    trick," said Sue and Scott. "We're going
    to make Spot vanish into thin air!"
"That's impossible!" said Molly.
"How will you do it?" asked Chris.
"That's our secret," said Scott.
"Well," said Molly, "whatever you do,
    you'd better not lose my dog."

A few days later the work was almost done.

Roger and Chris had built a stage.

They used old sheets and wooden boards.

"Watch where you're stepping!" Roger yelled
     as Sue tried to walk across the stage.

Sam was setting up chairs.

Sue was finishing the disappearing box.

Scott was digging and Spot was helping him.

They seemed to be making a big hole—or

maybe a tunnel?

Scott wouldn't say what they were doing.

He just said it was important for their trick.

Roger drew posters.

Chris tried to hang them up.

"Be careful! Or you'll bang that nail

right into my finger!" shouted Roger.

Everyone sold tickets.

Lots of kids on the block were interested
in magic, so ticket selling was pretty easy.

Finally everything was ready.

"I'm so nervous," said Sam.

"I'll do my trick first," said Molly.

"We'll save ours for last," said Sue.

# CHAPTER SIX

# SPOT STEALS THE SHOW

At 2 P.M. kids started arriving.

Sam collected their tickets.

Everyone took a seat.

Sue walked onto the stage.

"Quiet," she said, "the show is about to
        begin. I now present MOLLY THE MIND
        READER."

Molly walked onstage.

She closed her eyes and began. "My trick
        requires great concentration, so please
        be very quiet."

Molly slowly opened her eyes.

She asked a person from the audience to write a number between one and ten on a piece of paper.

Billy Maguire wrote a number.

When Billy handed the paper to Molly, she put it behind her back.

Everyone was quiet.

Suddenly Molly said, "I've got it! Your number is seven!"

"You're right!" said Billy. "How did you know the number I wrote?"

Molly did not tell her secret.

She bowed as the audience clapped.

Roger and Chris did their card tricks.

They were great.

Almost everybody was fooled.

Then Sam did the disappearing coin trick.

Everybody clapped and clapped.

This was a real magic show!

When Sam finished his trick, he waited
for everyone's attention.

Then he spoke: "Ladies and gentlemen,
for the most spectacular part of the
show, I now present SUE AND SCOTT
AND THE VANISHING SPOT!"

Sue brought the disappearing box onstage.

Scott and Spot followed.

Sue put the box down and Scott spoke:

"Here we have a regular wooden box."

Sue looked at Spot.

She said, "Spot, get into the box. Silence
in the audience, please."

Spot climbed into the box.

Scott made sure it was tightly closed.

Now for the magic wand and the magic words:

**PUDS! DUBS! SPUDS!**

Scott waved the wand and Sue clapped her hands twice.

Then Sue told Scott to open the box.

Everyone in the audience was surprised.

"He's really gone!" shouted a boy.

"Vanished!" said a girl.

"How did you do it?" called another.

Sue smiled, but she didn't answer.

Scott stepped forward and said:

"Since you're all wondering how we
did our last trick, just listen to
what Spot is saying. He's explaining
our secret!"